CHOOSE YOUR OWN ADVENTURE

We hope you enjoy reading this book. Every *Choose Your Own Adventure* story is about *you*! And every book is filled with choices that only *you* can make! You can keep reading and re-reading *Choose Your Own Adventure* books because every choice leads to a new adventure, so there are lots of ways for the stories to end.

All the titles currently available in the *Choose Your Own Adventure* series are listed on the page at the end of this book. You can buy them at your local branch of W H Smith, John Menzies, Martin the newsagent, Boots, at most good bookshops and local paperback stockists.

If you would like to know more about these books, or if you have difficulty obtaining any of them locally, or if you would like to tell us what you think of the series, write to: –

Choose Your Own Adventure,
Century House,
61–63 Uxbridge Road,
London W5 5SA.

CHOOSE YOUR OWN ADVENTURE® • 46

THE
DEADLY SHADOW

BY RICHARD BRIGHTFIELD

ILLUSTRATED BY DON HEDIN

An Edward Packard Book

BANTAM BOOKS
TORONTO • NEW YORK • LONDON • SYDNEY • AUCKLAND

RL 4, IL age 10 and up

THE DEADLY SHADOW
A Bantam Book / July 1985

*CHOOSE YOUR OWN ADVENTURE® is a registered trademark of
Bantam Books, Inc. Registered in U.S. Patent and Trademark
Office and elsewhere.*

Original conception of Edward Packard

ISBN 0-553-24991-6

Published simultaneously in the United States and Canada

Bantam Books are published by Bantam Books, Inc. Its trademark, consisting of the words "Bantam Books" and the por-
trayal of a rooster, is Registered in U.S. Patent and Trademark
Office and in other countries. Marca Registrada. Bantam
Books, Inc., 666 Fifth Avenue, New York, New York 10103.

Printed and bound in Great Britain by Hunt Barnard Printing Ltd.

O   0 9 8 7 6 5 4 3 2 1

To Judy Gitenstein

WARNING!!!

Do not read this book straight through from beginning to end! These pages contain many different adventures you may have as you search for the mysterious Dimitrius. From time to time, as you read along, you will be asked to make a choice. Your choice may lead to success or disaster.

The adventures you take are a result of your choice. *You* are responsible because *you* choose! After you make your choice, follow the instructions to see what happens to you next.

Think carefully before you make a decision. Remember: Dimitrius is extremely dangerous—and his shadow is deadly!

Good luck!

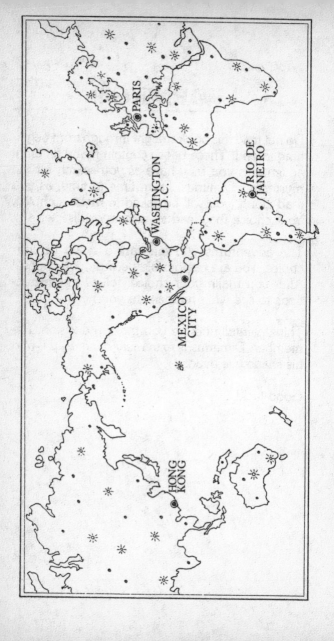

You are one of the top agents of the Special Security Agency (SSA). You have just returned from a successfully completed mission in the Far East. It is the first night of a promised and well deserved week of rest and relaxation, when the phone rings—at three in the morning.

It is your boss, "T," as he is known in the department. He wants you to come to Washington right away. Yes, he knows that you are supposed to get a short vacation after each assignment. But this is an emergency.

Wearily you pull yourself out of bed and get dressed. It is still dark outside when you jump into a cab and head for the airport, where you have your own small plane.

Dawn is just breaking over the Atlantic as you enter the landing pattern of a military airport just outside of Washington, D.C. You jog across the field, attaché case in hand, to a long dark-blue limousine waiting there for you.

You jump in and the limousine speeds off. T, a somber-looking man of fifty with a square face and a longish nose, is in the backseat.

"Sorry to interrupt your vacation," T says, "but this can't wait."

Turn to page 3.

The limo speeds across a bridge into downtown Washington, and soon stops in front of a nondescript office building. A uniformed guard appears and opens a side door, smartly saluting as you and T enter.

An elevator takes you down to a lower level and lets you out onto the platform of what looks like a miniature subway. The two of you step into a small bullet-shaped vehicle and sit down.

"This," says T, as the vehicle shoots forward, "will take us to a subterranean command post specially built for this operation."

Half an hour later you find yourself in a large underground room facing a wide, luminous world map. Dozens of red and green lights stand out on the map.

"Each one of those lights stands for a field operative searching for a man named Dimitrius," T explains.

"You mean that one man is so important that you have a huge operation like this just looking for him?" you ask.

Turn to page 5.

You follow Danielle through the kitchen to the alley door. You open it a crack and peer out. The alley is a dark, narrow passageway leading to the street. It is piled high with garbage cans and empty crates. It looks quiet.

"Let's go," you whisper.

With Danielle following, you move cautiously toward the tall rectangle of streetlight at the end. You are careful to stay hidden behind the packing crates as you inch forward. Suddenly the light is blocked by the hulking silhouette of a man—the man you saw get out of the car.

"Get as far back in the alley as you can," you whisper to Danielle.

You are not sure if the man sees you. Probably not, you think. Carefully you put down your attaché case and grab hold of a nearby trash can. It takes all of your strength to lift it. Just as the man sees you, you heave the garbage can at him. He casually bats the can aside with a gigantic fist—an oversize paw of metal that flashes in the streetlight. Then he quickly moves into the alley, trapping you against the brick wall behind you. You wonder how good his balance is as you roll another garbage can at his feet. The man stumbles forward, but his steel fist is coming directly toward your head.

Turn to page 55.

"He's not important," T answers. "He's dangerous—and now *you* will be searching for him."

"Why is he so dangerous?" you ask.

"Before I tell you that," says T, "I must swear you to the highest secrecy. On our side, other than the two of us, only the President and several of our leading scientists know the full truth about Dimitrius. What the Russians and the other countries know, I'm not sure . . . and they're not telling."

"What do we know?" you ask.

"Well, we know that Dimitrius was involved in a joint project of the Russian psychic research center in Moscow and the particle-physics laboratory at Noginsk."

"He's a Russian spy?"

"No, no!" exclaims T. "The Russians are as worried about him as we are."

"Worried that he'll do what?"

"That he may explode," says T with a sigh, sitting back down in his chair.

"Explode?" you repeat, wondering if T has lost his mind.

"Yes," says T hoarsely, "with the force of an atomic bomb."

"Are you sure?" you ask.

"That's what our scientists tell us," says T. "The original experiment performed with Dimitrius was to try to make him invisible. Apparently it also turned him into a human bomb. And there's more." T pauses and looks at you wearily. "Dimitrius may also be able to travel back and forth in time."

Turn to page 9.

You climb up the rope hand over hand, bracing your feet against the wall as you go up. At the top Big Fist grabs you and yanks you out of the window.

"This way, hurry!" he orders.

You are in a square courtyard. At the far side a low, arched gateway leads to the street. Following Big Fist, you dash toward it. Just beyond the gate, a car is waiting. You and Big Fist dive in, and the car roars away from the curb.

A familiar voice comes from the front seat. It's Jacques, your old friend in Paris—the one you were about to contact when you got the call from Danielle.

"Welcome back to Paris," Jacques says. "Looks like you had an adventurous night. Oh, by the way, your rescuer and companion in the backseat is Valon, my new assistant."

"Unfortunately I didn't know about him," you say, "otherwise I wouldn't have—"

"Just a misunderstanding," Valon interrupts. "You are wondering about my arm—yes?"

"Well, I . . ." you say.

"It was that devil Dimitrius," Valon says. "I tried to grab him just as he was starting to fade. I reached out, and my arm went through his shadow. It was as if my arm had plunged into a vat of molten metal. It was burned to a crisp."

"Then how . . . ?" you say.

Turn to page 16.

You and Juan climb down from the plane and watch as it takes off again. A battered open-backed truck drives out of a clump of tall bushes near the road and bounces onto the highway. You and Juan are shoved onto it. The kidnappers don't bother to tie you up, but four guards are sitting with you. Then the truck heads down the same stretch of highway that the plane used.

The truck drives on for hours. The air gets steadily hotter and more humid.

The guards sitting near you begin to doze. The driver and his companion in the front cab are staring straight ahead. You tap Juan on the shoulder, at the same time putting your finger to your lips. Then you point to the thick growth of vegetation along the side of the road.

Suddenly the truck jolts to a stop. A couple of mules are blocking the road. This could be the chance for you and Juan to jump off the truck and hide in the jungle. If the guards react too quickly, though, they could gun you down before you reach cover.

If you decide to make a run for it,
turn to page 84.

If you decide to stay in the truck,
turn to page 48.

T shows you the few pictures of Dimitrius that he has. As shown in the photos, Dimitrius is a short thin man with sharp features.

"Now take a look at the map," T says. "Each agent in the field carries a small transmitter that sends a signal relayed by satellite to this operations room, giving their position. If they find any trace of Dimitrius, they press a button that changes their light on the map from green to red."

"Has anyone found Dimitrius himself?" you ask.

"Not so far," says T, "but I'm depending on you to do just that. And remember, we just want to *talk* to Dimitrius. We don't want to harm him in any way—it might set him off. Now, let's decide on what undercover identity you'll assume on your search. For reasons that I'll explain later, I suggest a wealthy art collector or a professional gambler."

If you decide to assume the role of an art collector, turn to page 23.

If you decide to assume the role of a professional gambler, turn to page 74.

Danielle stands up and kicks your attaché case away from the base of the table. Two of the men in the club suddenly grab you from behind and drag you out of the chair. Suddenly you realize that this is not a real nightclub. Everyone in this room is an enemy agent!

A large sliding panel in the wall opens, revealing a brightly lit room. It looks like a scientific laboratory.

"Take the prisoner inside," Danielle says.

You are forced onto a table and quickly strapped down. Danielle jabs a hypodermic needle into your arm. At the same moment your head seems to explode.

Turn to page 29.

"Here's the letter," Juan says, handing it to Sandoz. "But my father's not going to believe it!"

"I don't care if he believes it or not," Sandoz replies. "He didn't believe me when I said that I didn't steal the famous crystal skull. It was taken by the ghosts of the Aztecs who made it. I may have taken a few little things from time to time, but nothing like the things your father has accused me of stealing."

"I believe you," you say.

"Oh, and just who are you?" asks Sandoz. "Besides being a meddling fool on the plane, as my men have told me."

"I am an agent of the American government," you say. "If you cooperate, I think I can clear you of—"

"Clear! Who cares about clear!" Sandoz exclaims. "I only care about my treasure. Come, I'll show you."

Sandoz leads you and Juan over to where an opening has been drilled in the side of the pyramid. He takes a flashlight and steps inside, gesturing for you to follow.

You descend a steep stairway that leads to a stone-vaulted chamber, far underground. Sandoz shines his flashlight around, illuminating piles of brilliant gold objects.

Go on to the next page.

"This is an ancient burial chamber," Sandoz says. "The gold in these pieces is worth a fortune. When they are melted down . . ."

"You can't destroy these treasures. They can't be replaced!" exclaims Juan. "That would be awful."

"I'll tell you what's awful," shouts Sandoz. "All these years I've helped dig up treasure and what did I get—nothing! This time it's going to be different."

"But, Sandoz—" you start.

"If you appreciate the treasure so much, you can spend some time with it," says Sandoz, pushing you and Juan into a small cell in the crypt. It has a recently constructed but heavy door. The door slams shut. You and Juan are plunged into darkness.

Turn to page 102.

A guard rushes up to Pollet. "The shadow!" he cries. "He's in the other gallery, and he's got his arms around the *Venus de Milo*."

"The *Venus de Milo*!" you exclaim. "You mean, the ancient Greek statue without arms?"

"That's the one!" says Pollet. "Hurry! There must be a way to stop him."

You race down the corridor with Pollet leading. Then suddenly you see something up ahead. It is the pale, ghostly shadow, seemingly floating in the air, of a man and a statue. You can see right through them. As you reach the spot they vanish completely.

"Don't just stand there!" Pollet shouts to the terrified guards. "We've got to do something!"

It takes a few minutes for Pollet to quiet down enough for you to ask him a question. "Have you had any night robberies, or anything like that, since the *Mona Lisa* was stolen?"

Turn to page 18.

"This arm is artificial—made of jointed steel and controlled electronically," Valon explains, pulling up his sleeve to show you.

"Then you know all about this Dimitrius," you say.

"Actually, we've been working for the SSA," Jacques says.

"But Danielle—where does she come in?" you ask.

"She's working for the Paris underworld," Jacques answers. "They are as interested in contacting Dimitrius as we are."

"What do they want Dimitrius for?" you ask. "For that matter, why *we* want him?"

"Dimitrius seems to have some uncanny abilities," Jacques says.

"Like making himself invisible?"

"That's part of it," says Jacques. "He also has a way of predicting the near future. He seems to know what is going to happen two or three weeks from now."

"This Dimitrius is strong—very strong," Valon puts in. "Somehow I absorbed some of his strength when I lost my real arm, trying to grab him. And, of course, his shadow is deadly."

"Are there any clues as to where he is now?" you ask.

Go on to the next page.

"Not many," says Jacques, "but there are two things that we know about him: He is a compulsive gambler and also an art thief. How he got involved with the Russian scientific experiments, we don't know."

"When we get to the Louvre," says Valon, "you will see what a thief he is. We are on our way there now."

"I'm going to the Louvre looking like this?" you say. "I just spent the night on a dirty cement floor."

"You don't look all that bad," says Valon, starting to brush off your clothes with his steel hand.

If you agree to go right to the Louvre,
turn to page 28.

If you insist on returning to the hotel,
turn to page 73.

"Well, we did have a midnight break-in about a week ago. The alarm system went off, but we never found the culprit, and nothing was taken."

"It could have been a break-*out* rather than a break-*in*," you say slowly. "I have a hunch that our friend Dimitrius somehow projects himself into the future along with his stolen goods."

"You are talking about time travel?" Pollet asks.

"Yes," you say, "Dimitrius may enter a different dimension. And I'm guessing that once he's returned to the present, he can't just slip into the future. Or maybe he doesn't have any real control over it. This spot is like a gate that he has to go through—into the future or back to the present. If I'm right, Dimitrius will be back; and not only that, he will have accumulated a tremendous amount of atomic energy from his trip through time."

"*Atomic* energy!" Pollet exclaims. "You mean like in atomic bombs?"

"Similar, though perhaps not as powerful—yet!" you say. "We can either try to contain that energy or try to neutralize it."

"How can we do that?" asks Pollet.

"A heavy steel cage might contain the energy, though I can't say for certain," you reply. "A lot of water might neutralize it, but I'm not sure of that either."

If you recommend that the museum construct a steel cage around the spot, turn to page 82.

If you recommend that guards stand by with fire hoses, turn to page 75.

Something about Danielle's call intrigues you. Taking your attaché case, you head for the Café Le Dôme. You have no trouble spotting Danielle. You walk over to her table on the sidewalk.

"I'm so glad that you came," Danielle says. "It's very important that I find this Dimitrius."

"Welcome to the club," you say, "but I know almost nothing about him myself, except that he has everyone in a tizzy."

"*Mais oui,*" she says. "I believe you, but . . ."

Danielle's eyes shift to a black Citroën slowly cruising by on the boulevard. She gives a start, and her pale gray eyes open wide.

"It was a mistake meeting you here in the open," she says. "There are people who would like to eliminate both of us."

You see that the Citroën has stopped a little way down the block, and a giant of a man is getting out of the back. Suddenly Danielle gestures for you to follow and runs into the café.

Go on to the next page.

"The owner of this café is a friend of mine," she explains. "We can either go out through the kitchen door into the back alley, or we can hide in the wine cellar."

*If you decide to flee into the alley,
turn to page 4.*

*If you decide to hide in the wine cellar,
turn to page 72.*

The cab stops on a narrow street in the Latin Quarter. You don't see anything remotely resembling the entrance to a club, but Danielle leads you into a dark doorway and then down a long corridor lit by a single yellow bulb. At the end of the hallway you reach a stairway leading down. Then you hear the murmuring sounds of the club—laughing, talking, and accordion music. At the bottom of the stairs you push aside a beaded curtain. You are in a candlelit, smoky room with a vaulted ceiling. Crowded tables are spaced along the wall. In the center, sitting on a stool, is the accordion player. Danielle directs you to a corner table.

"Now tell me where Dimitrius is," Danielle says. In the light of the candle on the table her face has taken on a sinister look.

"But that's what I flew to Paris to try to find out!" you protest.

"I don't believe you," Danielle says. There is a small revolver in her hand—pointed directly at you. You are not sure what is going on, but you can feel the edge of your attaché case against your foot. If you can divert her attention for a second, you can push the table over on her and get to your attaché case.

If you decide to try to stop Danielle, turn to page 63.

If you decide to wait and see what she is going to do, turn to page 10.

"The role of an art collector, particularly a rich one, sounds good to me," you say. "I can travel in the style to which I would like to become accustomed."

"This time you're lucky," says T. "No expense is being spared for this search. But I expect every penny to be accounted for when you turn in your final report."

"Don't worry about that," you say with a smile, "just give me my first destination."

"Let's see," mutters T to himself as he gazes at the map. "There are red signals from both Paris and Mexico City, where Dimitrius has surfaced in connection with the art world. It seems that he is a bit of a collector himself."

"This Dimitrius really gets around," you say.

"More than you can imagine," says T. "But now you have your choice between these two places. And by the way, I suggest that you take your special attaché case. You'll need every trick in it."

If you decide to go to Mexico City,
turn to page 26.

If you decide to go to Paris, turn to page 32.

Seventeen hours later you are aboard a jet as it glides slowly earthward. You recognize the lights of Hong Kong laid out like sparkling strings of jewels around the harbor. Far below, bursts of fireworks from a celebration open into multicolored petals of light.

After going through customs, you look around for your SSA contact in Hong Kong. You wait for an hour, then decide to telephone your old friend Lu Chang, who lives in nearby Kawloon, the mainland city just across the channel from Hong Kong Island. Lu also works for the SSA on occasion.

No one answers Lu's phone. You decide to go over to his place and wait for him.

You arrive in downtown Kawloon by cab and quickly find a ricksha. Somehow rickshas can thread their way through the teeming streets even faster than you could on foot.

Lu's book and record shop is on Nathan Road, the main shipping street in Kawloon. There is only a small boy inside watching the store. You know that Lu lives in a small apartment off the rear of the store. You ask for Lu, and the boy points to a door in the back. As you enter the apartment you see a group of people standing around the bed. The person lying on the bed is completely wrapped in bandages.

Somehow you know it is Lu. You run over to your friend.

"What happened?" you ask.

Turn to page 41.

You and Juan cross the streambed and work your way through the thick vegetation on the other side. You push steadily upward for a while and then come to a path.

"It will probably take us to a village sooner or later," you say.

You and Juan continue to hike along the path. Occasionally through the trees you catch a glimpse of the mountains up ahead. Then you come to a strange section of the jungle where many of the trees and undergrowth have been stripped of their leaves.

"Something cut a wide path through here," you say. "I wonder what it was."

"Looks like the work of army ants," Juan says with a shiver. "When they migrate, they cut a swath through the jungle, devouring everything in their path—plants and even animals."

"You mean a bunch of little ants did this?" you exclaim.

"They're not so little," Juan replies. "Some of them are almost an inch long. They have razor-sharp pincers that can take a hunk of flesh right out of you. And when they're migrating, there are thousands of them."

"I'm glad they've gone by already," you say. "I'd hate to tangle with them."

Night falls, and you make camp the best you can by the side of the trail. Exhausted, you both go right to sleep. But in the middle of the night a sharp pain in your foot wakes you up. There is a buzzing all around you in the jungle.

Turn to page 117.

After the briefing, you head straight for Dulles International Airport to catch a flight to Mexico City.

About halfway to the airport you look out of the back window of your cab. You don't know if it is your imagination, but a large gray car seems to be following you. Or perhaps the driver is just going to the airport as you are.

You're not going to take any chances. At the airport you duck into a side doorway of the terminal. A few seconds later the gray car pulls up to the curb. Two men get out and stand there for a few moments, whispering to each other. One of them is short and has a heavy mustache like the old-time bandit Pancho Villa. The other is taller and thinner. They go into the front entrance of the terminal building.

You slip out of your hiding place and follow the men to the ticket counter inside the terminal. You watch them buy tickets and then head for the main waiting area. You go up to the counter and flash your SSA credentials for the clerk.

"Those two men who just bought tickets," you say, "where are they going?"

"They are taking the next flight to Mexico City," the clerk answers.

Now, isn't that a coincidence? you think.

"Give me a ticket for the same flight," you say.

Turn to page 96.

Jacques heads straight for the center of Paris, where the vast Louvre museum, one of the largest in the world, sprawls along the north bank of the River Seine.

You follow Jacques and Valon through a side entrance in one of the museum's long wings. The curator's office is at the end of cavernous corridor that reminds you that this was once an imperial palace.

"This is Monsieur Pollet," Jacques says, introducing you to the curator. "I'll let him tell you his story."

"Three weeks ago," starts Pollet, "a man entered the museum along with the regular visitors and . . . but let me show you."

Turn to page 38.

That's all you remember until you wake up with a splitting headache. You are lying on the floor in a bare room made of stone that looks like a deep pit. A solid metal door is set in one of the walls, and high above a gleam of light filters through a solitary barred window. You lie there for a while, trying to get your head back together. Suddenly a shadow moves across the outside of the window above. You look up and see a large steel hand grab hold of the bars. There is a grinding sound as the hand tears the bars from the window. A head appears. No mistaking it, it's Big Fist. The head disappears but a rope comes snaking down from above.

"Hurry!" shouts a deep voice from above.

What now? you think. If you follow Big Fist's orders, you may be going from the frying pan into the fire, as they say—or worse.

If you decide to take a chance and climb the rope, turn to page 6.

If you decide to stay where you are, turn to page 59.

"Let's get far away from here," Juan whispers.

"I'm not sure I should leave Dimitrius," you say.

Then two things happen. Sandoz and his men rush up the pyramid after Dimitrius. At the same moment a bolt of lightning shoots down from the sky, squarely hitting Dimitrius, who is now at the very top. His figure lights up with a brilliant incandescence—then it seems to grow to twice its size, sending a cascading fountain of sparks down the pyramid. His deep voice booms out, louder than the thunder crashing in the background. "I know all . . . I see all . . . I am all-powerful . . . I am . . ."

Dimitrius's voice rises in pitch until it becomes an unearthly scream. The entire pyramid below him is now glowing as if it were hot enough to melt and flow away as lava. Your hair is literally standing on end—either from fright or some overcharged electrical disturbance in the air.

"Run! Run!" you gasp. You grab Juan and pull him away from the horrible but fascinating scene.

You and Juan race down the trail, the roar behind you growing louder and louder. You run for a long while, then a titanic explosion lifts you into the air and hurls you to the ground. Fortunately you are both thrown into a deep ditch that saves you from the force of the blast. You lie there trembling as fragments of rock rip through the jungle for miles around.

When you are able to raise your head and look back, you see a column of flame rising into the sky.

Turn to page 114.

That evening, you are met at Orly airport by a man who introduces himself as the local SSA agent. You've barely squeezed your attaché case into his tiny sports car before he heads toward the center of the city.

"What's the evidence that Dimitrius is in Paris?" you ask.

"He *was* in Paris," says the agent. "I'm sure of it. But then, he seems to be all over the place—all at the same time."

"Then he really can travel in time?"

"That's just one of his talents. He can also make himself invisible, and when he disappears . . ." The agent shakes his head. "I don't even believe it. Anyway, Dimitrius himself is only half the problem. The rest of the danger comes from everyone else involved."

"You mean, the Russians," you say.

"The KGB, the Paris criminal underworld, a band of Chinese assassins, and assorted terrorist groups—to name a few—are out scouring for any trace of Dimitrius."

Go on to the next page.

"Well, if Dimitrius can actually make himself invisible, there's no telling what he can do. Are you sure that he—"

"Let me take you to the Louvre museum," says the agent. "The curator is working late tonight. I want you to hear *his* story for yourself."

"Tonight? Right now?" you ask. "I'm pretty tired. Why don't you let me get a good night's sleep, and we'll go see this guy first thing in the morning?"

Actually you want to contact your own private source of information in Paris before you talk to anyone else.

"But every minute counts!" says the agent.

If you decide to go straight to the hotel, turn to page 44.

If you decide to go see the curator, turn to page 57.

As you wait to see what the hijackers do, you feel the plane change course and start to descend. The taller man appears at the door of the flight deck.

"If everyone behaves themselves," he says, "the plane will land safely, we will leave, and you will be allowed to take off again for Mexico City."

You look out of the window over Juan's shoulders. Where are they going to land? Then you see it—a long, straight stretch of deserted highway cutting across a relatively flat area.

Not long after, the plane touches down, bouncing a couple of times before coming to a stop.

"We are leaving now—*adiós*," says the man in front, opening the outside door of the plane. "And this boy is coming with us," he adds, coming back to your seat and waving his pistol at Juan.

"I'm not going anywhere," Juan protests.

"Oh, yes, you are!" says the man, reaching over you for Juan.

You grab the man by the arm and send him crashing down the aisle into the man with the mustache. At the same time you manage to grab the taller man's gun. For a moment you have the advantage. Unfortunately several men from outside the plane jump on board, pointing submachine guns at you. You have no choice but to let go of the kidnappers.

"No more tricks," says the taller man as he pulls himself up. "And now both of you are coming out," he says, pointing his gun first at Juan and then at you.

Turn to page 8.

"Dimitrius needs our help," you tell T.

"Splendid," T says. "The important thing now is to get him into orbit in space."

"Into orbit!" exclaims Dimitrius, who is listening in on an extension phone.

"Yes," T says. "Our physicists have determined that by traveling between the future and the present, you may be building up an enormous explosive potential. You could blow up with the force of an atom bomb at any moment. Luckily we have been secretly building a space station laboratory that will remain in orbit with you—if you're willing—until we can figure out how to reverse the condition. I'm afraid it's the only safe place for you."

"Then I must get there before I start to fade again," says Dimitrius. "I have only so much control over it."

You thank Mai Ling for her help. Then you and Dimitrius take off for Hong Kong, where a U.S. Army transport waits to take the two of you directly to Cape Canaveral. Dimitrius's space shuttle is being readied for takeoff there.

T is waiting for you on the Cape. "Good work," he says, shaking your hand.

"Thanks, T," you say. "Now, how about my vacation?"

"Certainly," says T. "As soon as you return from your next little mission.

"As you know, Dimitrius is in a volatile state," T explains smoothly. "We feel it's important that he have someone along whom he trusts. You'll get your vacation as soon as you return from orbit."

The End

You all follow Pollet, up a flight of marble stairs and down a long gallery lined with portraits, to one special painting at the far end. The painting is protected by a thick plate of glass, but you recognize it immediately—the *Mona Lisa,* Leonardo da Vinci's most famous painting.

"This is a copy," whispers Pollet. "A good one—but still a copy."

"What happened to the original?" you ask.

"Three weeks ago it was still here. Then this man pulled it off the wall, frame and all," says Pollet. "And then he—and the painting—started to fade. One of the guards rushed over and struck at his vanishing shadow; the club went right through it. The guard was about to strike again, but the tip of his club that was *in* the shadow had already disintegrated! So the guard ran for help, but by the time he returned with others, the man and the *Mona Lisa* were gone."

"This seems to be Dimitrius's method of operation," Jacques says. "He's stolen the most famous paintings from major museums around the world."

Just at that moment the museum's alarm bell goes off.

Turn to page 15.

You and Juan hurry down the streambed, trying to put as much distance as you can between yourselves and the kidnappers.

You go on for hours. Fortunately there's some shade under the trees, the tops of which hang like umbrellas high over the dry stream. But it is humid and very hot. It is not long before you are both exhausted.

"I'm still worried about this streambed," Juan says. "I thought I just heard thunder."

"But it's completely clear overhead," you say. "Look over there through the trees. There's not a cloud in the sky."

"There could be rainstorms in the mountains," Juan says. "That gives me an uneasy feeling."

"Speaking of feeling," you say, "my legs are numb. I have to rest for a while."

"Okay," Juan agrees, "but no longer than we have to." He sits down and closes his eyes.

You slump down against a rock. All thoughts about Dimitrius and your primary mission have been forgotten. You are conscious only of the heat and the insects buzzing around your head.

For a few minutes the jungle seems to become strangely still. Then you hear a roaring sound—almost like a locomotive—and it's getting closer. A train in this part of the jungle? you ask yourself. It's possible, but—

You jump to your feet and shake Juan. "Quick!" you shout. "We've got to get out of here!"

Turn to page 80.

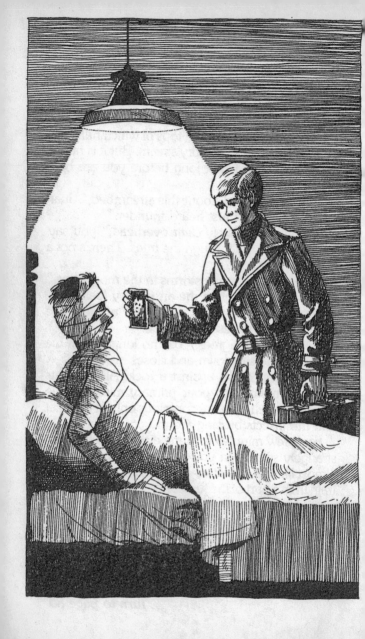

"At the Happy Valley Racetrack on Hong Kong Island," Lu says in a muffled voice, "the SSA told me to watch for anyone having extraordinary luck. There was this man . . . everyone at the betting windows was amazed at his winning streak. He never lost. Finally he left in a limousine with two guards dressed all in black. I followed on my bicycle to a villa high up on Victoria Peak. I watched all day from what I thought was a safe distance. Just after dark the two men in black jumped me from behind. They dragged me into the villa. The man with the winning streak was there."

"Is this him?" you ask, holding up a photo of Dimitrius. Painfully Lu pushes himself up to look.

"That's him, all right!" Lu sinks back on the bed. "He came toward me. As he did, it seemed, crazily enough, that he was starting to fade. I could see right through him. Then, when he reached me, I felt like I had been tossed into a bonfire. I passed out screaming. Later they must have dumped me into the harbor. The cold water revived me just enough for me to swim to shore. Someone found me and got an ambulance. I was burned over most of my body."

"Do you remember where this villa is?" you ask.

"I can give you directions to it," says Lu, "but I would not go there again. And you may get more information at the racetrack."

If you try to find the villa, turn to page 49.

If you decide to go to the Happy Valley Racetrack in Hong Kong, turn to page 58.

You and Juan bang on the door as hard as you can. Then you look through the peephole again. You can see Dimitrius's startled expression.

"Dimitrius!" you shout. "I represent the American government. They just want to talk!"

Dimitrius lets out a fiendish laugh. "Of course, they want to talk to me. They *all* want to talk to me. They want to know the source of my power."

Still holding his loot, Dimitrius grabs hold of your cell door and rips it off.

"He didn't even undo the latch first," Juan says in amazement.

"You see!" Dimitrius shouts, and heads up the stairs. You and Juan follow cautiously.

It's dark outside. A rumble of thunder in the distance signals that a tropical storm is about to begin. At first you can't find Dimitrius; then you see his luminous form halfway up the pyramid. For a moment he seems to slip a bit and drops one of the heavy gold objects. It goes clanging down the steep steps of the pyramid. Shouts go up all around the camp as Sandoz's men hear the noise and catch sight of Dimitrius. Sandoz himself comes running out.

"My treasure!" shouts Sandoz. "Someone is stealing my treasure!"

Sandoz's voice is echoed by a clap of thunder rolling across the jungle. Seconds later a flash of lightning further illuminates Dimitrius. Sandoz's men fire their guns wildly at him—with no effect. In the excitement no one notices you and Juan slipping away.

Turn to page 31.

You go alone to the Maracanã Stadium. Isabel is checking on some leads downtown. The stadium is packed—sold out. People are fighting to get in. The fans outside are in a state of near riot. You wonder if you'll be able to get in to the game.

Still, if Dimitrius is here at all, he is as likely to be hanging around outside the stadium as inside. You search the crowd. Every once in a while you spot someone who looks like Dimitrius from a distance. But then, when you struggle through the crowd, it turns out to be somebody else.

You are getting deeper and deeper into the throng. The crush is terrific—you can barely hold on to your attaché case. Then someone near the base of the stadium wall shouts that there is a way open to the inside. There is a sudden mass rush in that direction. You are knocked to the ground. Thousands of hysterical fans stampede over you.

What a terrible way for an SSA agent to go— trampled to death at a soccer game.

The End

"Just drop me off at the hotel, and we'll talk in the morning," you tell the agent.

At the hotel a bellhop takes your bags up to your luxury penthouse suite. You are careful to carry your attaché case yourself. It contains your most important spying devices.

You step outside onto your terrace. Down below is the wide sweep of the Champs-Élysées, the most elegant boulevard in Paris. To one side the Eiffel Tower rises in all its splendor, and in the other direction the city climbs up a hillside to the floodlit brilliance of the church of the Sacré-Cœur.

You go back into your suite, open your attaché case, and take out the telephone scrambler. It converts any conversation into a meaningless jumble of sounds unless someone has a similar device to unscramble the message at the other end. You are about to attach it to the mouthpiece of the phone when the phone rings.

Turn to page 52.

"They say that Dimitrius travels into the future, reads the newspapers, finds out who won, and then returns to the present," Isabel tells you.

"Do you really believe that?" you ask.

"Well, strange things happen with this Dimitrius," she says with a shrug. "A few weeks back a rival gang of gamblers ambushed him. They tried to shoot him, but Dimitrius turned into some kind of . . . shadow—a deadly shadow. Bullets had no effect, and when one man tried to grab him, the gangster burst into flames."

"This gang that pays Dimitrius for information," you say, "how do they contact him?"

"From what I've been able to find out," Isabel says, "they meet at the top of Sugarloaf Mountain. I don't know exactly when. There is a *fút*—excuse me—soccer game this afternoon. They could be meeting today. A lot of gambling money is riding on this game. It is the the World Cup—the biggest prize in soccer. It is possible that Dimitrius will show up at the stadium."

If you decide to look for Dimitrius on the top of Sugarloaf Mountain, turn to page 69.

If you decide to go to the stadium, turn to page 43.

"Dimitrius!" you exclaim.

"That's right," he says, waving his gun, "and now I suggest that we return to the villa."

"Look, Dimitrius," you say, "I've been trying to find you. I'm here as an agent of the American government. They just want to talk to you."

"The *American* government?" says Dimitrius.

"That's right," you say.

"Why should I believe you?" Dimitrius asks. "But I sense you are telling the truth. I'm going to trust you, but you'll have to trust me. Fly this helicopter to my yacht, and I'll contact your government from there."

If you decide to trust Dimitrius and fly to his yacht, turn to page 111.

If you don't trust him and fly toward the Hong Kong harbor police headquarters, turn to page 78.

You and Juan decide to stay in the truck. The mules are pulled off the road by their owners, and the truck picks up speed.

"I wish I knew what this is all about," Juan whispers to you. "My family doesn't have a lot of money. My father is the director of the National Anthropological Museum in Mexico City, but he doesn't make that much."

Director of a museum—that's interesting, you think. "Have there been any major thefts from the museum recently?" you ask.

"There certainly have been," says Juan. "My father was in Washington last month for a conference on museum thefts. He said that there are similar art thefts going on all over the world."

"Similar? In what way?"

"Well, this will sound strange to you," says Juan, "but I heard my father say they were all done by a ghostlike figure—a kind of shadow. I also heard him talking about somebody called Dimitrius."

"What did he say about Dimitrius?" you ask.

"I can't remember much," answers Juan. "My father thinks that a man named Sandoz, an archaeologist that used to work for the museum, is involved—maybe even working with this Dimitrius."

At the mention of Sandoz one of the guards opens his eyes wide and sits up.

"You will do no more talking," he orders.

The truck comes to a stop, and the two men in the cab get out and run to the back of the truck.

Turn to page 85.

The next day you ferry across the harbor to Hong Kong Island. You hire a taxi and set off in search of the villa that Lu Chang told you about. You have no trouble finding it, but you don't want to get too close and be ambushed the way Lu was.

The ornate, rambling house is on a high hill surrounded by woods. You have the cab stop some distance away and carefully work your way toward the villa on foot. Once into the woods you slip slowly forward, keeping an eye out for any alarm sensors that might be planted. You have activated your own heat-sensing alarm in your attaché case. Any man or animal nearby will make it give a barely audible click.

You are crouched behind a tree halfway through the woods, scanning the villa windows with your binoculars, when you hear the ominous click of your sensor. Then comes another click with a slightly different tone. You realize that you are being approached from several directions: You are surrounded!

You look around. Shadowy figures are darting through the woods toward you. You think you see a way past them. You make a run for it. Suddenly you trip over a wire. There is a loud explosion, and you lose consciousness.

Turn to page 98.

In Hong Kong, Ho leads you to the waterfront and introduces you to his friend Ahn, who owns a small but fast motorboat.

"I must stay behind," explains Ho, "but I will tell Ahn how to find this island."

The boat zips away from the pier and heads south.

"I think I know the island you are looking for," says Ahn. "It used to be a base for smugglers."

After an hour of bouncing over the waves and threading your way through dozens of small islands, two powerboats roar out from behind one of the islands and speed toward you.

"Why are they racing here?" you ask. "There isn't that much room to maneuver."

"Those aren't racers." Ahn's voice is grim. "Those are smugglers' boats. They must think we're rival smugglers, and they're trying to cut us off."

Your boat swerves hard away from the rapidly approaching boats. You can see a small cannon on the bow of the closest one. A puff of smoke rises from it. Moments later, a geyser of water from the shell jets up in front of you. Then another. Ahn steers a wild zigzagging course to keep the smugglers from zeroing in on you.

Suddenly a shot hits your gas tank. A huge ball of orange flame envelops your boat, and bits of burning debris from the explosion rocket into the sky. No one ever finds Dimitrius—and this is the last trace of you.

The End

"Hello?" you say.

"Hello," says a soft woman's voice with a slight French accent. "My name is Danielle Picot. I represent certain mutual interests—that is, if you are interested in finding a certain individual whose name I won't mention on the phone."

"How did you get my name?" you ask. "And how—"

"We have our inside sources," she interrupts, laughing, "even inside your government's SSA."

"And what government are *you* working for?" you ask.

"This thing is bigger than any government," she says, a note of indignation entering her voice. "If you want to exchange information, I am at the Café Le Dôme on Avenue de la Bourdonnais. I'm wearing a black turtleneck with a string of pearls. My hair is blond. You can't miss me."

"But I don't have any infor—" you begin. A click tells you that she has hung up.

If you decide to meet Danielle, turn to page 19.

If you decide to contact your source in Paris instead, turn to page 118.

Red wins. You've won a fortune. You go over to the cashier's window and cash in your chips for Hong Kong dollars—a million of them. You suddenly realize that you never have to work for the SSA again.

You register in a *very* fancy hotel and send a cable to T saying that you resign. Then you settle down to enjoy spending your money—on yourself!

The End

You dive to one side as the man's metal fist whistles by your head and into the brick wall behind you. The fist goes right through the wall. You grab another garbage can and throw it at his back. His arm goes into the wall up to his shoulder. Then the man wheels around, tearing out part of the wall and bringing down a shower of bricks on his head. He brushes them aside like confetti.

You crawl around on the ground and find your attaché case. Quickly you turn the combination lock to number six and press down on a concealed button. A burst of green gas shoots out of the end of the attaché case and envelops Big Fist's head just as he starts toward you again. The green gas is an anesthetic developed by the SSA that is strong enough to stop an elephant. You hold your breath for the sixty seconds that the gas is active.

Big Fist just stands there. For a moment you are afraid that the gas won't work. Then he topples over and crashes into a large pile of empty boxes. Big Fist will be out for an hour. You stumble back to where Danielle is crouching in the shadows.

"Quick!" you exclaim. "Let's get out of here."

Turn to page 62.

Dimitrius, startled, turns and starts to run to the back of the chopper. Instantly you understand Mai Ling's strategy. You don't like to do it, but it's a matter of survival. You hope Mai Ling is holding on tight as you throw the helicopter into a sharp starboard bank. From the rear you hear a scream as Dimitrius loses his footing and falls through the open cargo door into space. Then you right the helicopter.

"Mai Ling, are you okay?" you holler.

Mai Ling comes back into the cockpit. "Guess we took care of him," she says.

"I just hope he can swim," you say. "My government still wants to talk to him."

You turn the helicopter around and head back over the spot where Dimitrius hit the water.

"There he is," you say. "And there's another boat heading for him!"

Turn to page 60.

"Good," says the agent, with a sigh. "We'll stop off on the way to the Louvre and switch to the agency's limousine."

"Limousine?" you say.

"Oh, yes," says the agent, "bulletproof, you know. Just an extra precaution. I'm afraid that there are others who know that you were sent here to look for Dimitrius. Others who will stop at nothing to find him first."

"You mean, there's a leak in the agency?"

The agent laughs bitterly. "I'm afraid so."

"This thing really is rough," you say.

"Rougher than you know," mutters the agent.

After a short drive the agent pulls behind a limousine parked on a side road. You get out and walk to the limo. The agent holds the door open as you get in. Then, instead of getting in himself, he slams the door shut—locking you inside.

Turn to page 83.

To the racetrack it is. You are back out on bustling Nathan Road with its gleaming red double-decker buses and its bright neon signs. A ricksha takes you to the ferry. You have to cross Victoria Harbor to get to Hong Kong Island and the Happy Valley Racecourse.

Once on the ferry you go up to the top deck to take in the spectacular harbor scene. Out of the side of your eye, you notice several Chinese following you. They are all dressed in black—something not unusual in itself, but you sense immediately that they belong to an ancient order of professional assassins. You've tangled with this group before and felt yourself lucky to come out of it alive. One of them is heading your way, warily but quickly.

Turn to page 112.

You crouch in the corner of the pitlike room, ignoring the now angry shouts coming from Big Fist above.

"Hurry! Hurry!" he repeats. "They'll be on to us in a few moments."

Then there is the sound of gunfire from somewhere outside—beyond Big Fist and the window.

"Aghhh . . ." cries Big Fist. Then he swings inside the window and starts to slide down the rope. Halfway down he loses his grip and crashes to the floor beside you.

Turn to page 106.

You watch to see if they fish him out of the water. But before the boat can reach him, a whirlpool starts to form around Dimitrius. Not only that, a column of steam rises from the center of it. You can't see Dimitrius anymore, but a pool of flame starts to fill the center of the rapidly growing whirlpool.

The boat that was heading for Dimitrius wheels around and flees. Then the whole scene is hidden by thick clouds of smoke and steam. You watch horrified as occasional flashes of fire shine through. A continuous sound like thunder booms across the bay for several minutes. Then silence.

The wind blows away the smoke, revealing a calm sea beneath. There is no sign of Dimitrius.

"That guy sure knows how to make an exit," you say.

"Do you think that's the end of him?" asks Mai Ling.

"I don't know," you say, "but I have a feeling that Dimitrius took a really long trip in time—this time."

The End

With Danielle in tow you go back down to the street and hail a cab. You and Danielle climb inside.

You're beginning to wonder just how Danielle is connected to the search for Dimitrius. "Now I should really get back to the hotel," you say. "Between that fight with Big Fist and jet lag, I'm ready for some sleep."

"Oh, no!" exclaims Danielle. "It's vital that I talk to you. Just give me another half hour. I know an underground nightclub in the Latin Quarter. We can talk there without being disturbed."

If you decide to go to the Latin Quarter with Danielle, turn to page 22.

If you decide to go back to the hotel, turn to page 115.

You look over your shoulder and fake a surprised look.

"You don't think I'm going to fall for that old trick, do you?" Danielle says.

But fall for it or not, it does make her hesitate for a vital split second. You lift up the table and shove it toward her. Danielle's gun fires, but the bullet is deflected by the hard slate tabletop. At the same time you make a dive for the attaché case at your feet.

In a second you have your stun pistol in your hand and are firing at Danielle, who is now trying to pull herself out from under the table. The blast from your gun knocks her out. You spring to your feet and make a run for the door.

You never make it. The accordion player's instrument hides a gun. He stops playing and starts firing.

The End

Early the next morning you are on a jet gliding in low over the turquoise waters of Guanabara Bay—ringed with the pearl-white sands of Rio's famous beaches.

Soon you are in the center of the modern, dazzling city that is Rio de Janeiro—River of January. Not that you haven't been here before—you have, many times. You check into your favorite hotel not far from Copacabana Beach. There is a letter for you at the desk. It is from your SSA contact in Rio, a new one since you were here last. You are to meet your contact at the racetrack in an hour.

You are waiting around the betting windows, reviewing your code words, when a slim, dark-haired woman asks, "Do you know when the next race will start?"

"I just arrived here myself," you answer, giving the first part of a prearranged code.

"In that case," she says, "we should go and find out when it is to begin."

Turn to page 68.

You are the only one on the plane still conscious. The others will be asleep for the next hour or so. You run to the pilot's compartment. The plane is on automatic pilot—so no worry there. You go back to your attaché case and find a small glass vial. You take it back to the flight deck and break it under the pilot's nose. He revives immediately. You explain the situation, and he goes back with you to help tie up the hijackers.

Later you land at the Mexico City airport. The hijackers are turned over to the police. An urgent telegram from T is waiting for you:

CHANGE IDENTITY TO THAT OF GAMBLER. PROCEED IMMEDIATELY TO HONG KONG. CONTACT LOCAL SSA AGENT HO LING.

Turn to page 24.

You and Mai Ling quickly climb into the back of the truck, closing the rear doors behind you. You crouch behind the large empty wooden tubs that still smell of fish. Seconds later the truck starts off.

After a few minutes of traveling Mai Ling whispers, "We will soon be at the waterfront."

"We'll jump out the next time the truck slows down," you whisper back.

Soon it does, and both of you slip out. The truck speeds away, and the two of you cross the street to the front of a large ornate building. A sign says FU LOONG CASINO.

Suddenly you remember something—you feel along your waist. Your money belt is still there under your clothes. Well, you're supposed to be a professional gambler, and here is a casino. Maybe you'll find a clue to Dimitrius. You decide to go in and try your luck.

Turn to page 77.

As you walk she introduces herself. "My name is Isabel Alvorada. I just started at this a few weeks ago." She smiles. "I see that you have your famous attaché case with you."

"I didn't realize it was so famous," you say.

"Just within the SSA, of course," she says. "It was the first thing they told me about you."

"Do you know much about this Dimitrius?"

"He is not so hard to find," Isabel replies, laughing. "He is often in Rio. He is well-known in certain circles . . . gambling circles."

"I take it that Dimitrius likes to bet on the races," you say.

"The races," Isabel repeats. "Yes . . . sometimes. But he mostly bets on *fútbol*."

"Ah, you mean soccer," you say. "In the States our football is a completely different game."

"Soccer, as you say," Isabel goes on. "This Dimitrius always knows who is going to win—always! At first the gamblers bet against him until they learned their lesson. Now one group of gamblers pays Dimitrius large sums of money to predict who is going to win."

"Do you have any idea how Dimitrius knows?" you ask.

Isabel leans close to you and whispers.

Turn to page 46.

With Isabel you head for Sugarloaf Mountain. A cable car is thrilling anywhere in the world, but the ride to the top of this mountain is something special. At the top you and Isabel walk around the main viewing area, trying to blend in with the tourists. The panorama is spectacular, with hundreds of soaring mountaintops casting their shadows across the sparkling bay.

Gradually you work your way onto the side paths. On one of the narrower paths you notice a group of suspicious-looking men. Gangsters, you think.

The group winds down the path. You and Isabel follow at a distance and watch a man step out of the trees and approach the group. Even at this distance you recognize him. It's Dimitrius.

Dimitrius and the gangsters are talking earnestly. Suddenly a second group of men run toward the ones you are watching. Both groups pull out guns and start firing. Some topple to the ground. The bullets seem to have no effect on Dimitrius.

Go on to the next page.

Dimitrius simply walks through the gunfire, heading toward you and Isabel. Two of the gangsters stumble to their feet as Dimitrius walks right past you.

"Dimitrius!" you shout, "I have to talk to you."

Turn to page 109.

Danielle leads you down to the wine cellar below the café. It is larger than you expected. There are rows and rows of barrels on one side and aisles of neatly stacked bottles on the other. You and Danielle move quickly to the far end of the cellar and duck down behind a row of barrels. Moments later you hear heavy footsteps approaching.

Danielle points to a trap door in the floor. "This leads to one of the drainage tunnels of the sewers. It is large enough for us to walk through, and I'm sure there is a ladder to the street. But we must hurry if we are to escape."

You lift the trap door as quietly as possible. Danielle goes first. You follow, carefully closing the trap door behind you. It is pitch-dark in the tunnel, but you manage to fish out a flashlight from your attaché case. As the beam stabs down the tunnel you see Danielle hurrying away. You follow as quickly as you can, sloshing along in water up to your ankles.

"It's not far now," Danielle calls, her voice echoing hollowly through the tunnel.

Suddenly there is a strong blast of air through the tunnel, and you hear a roaring behind you.

Turn to page 93.

When you return to the hotel, you find someone waiting for you in the lobby. A short, balding man with large steel-rimmed glasses approaches you. "I am Professor Savenson," he says, sounding quite nervous. "I got your name from the SSA in Washington—from your boss, T, as I believe you refer to him. I must talk to you in private. It concerns this man you are looking for."

You are not sure that you should trust Savenson, but then this mission has been strange from the start. You'll take another chance.

"Come up to my room and we'll discuss it," you say.

Minutes later Savenson is pacing the floor of your room.

"Now, what is it that I can do for you?" you ask.

"This man, Dimitrius, must be found at all costs," Savenson says.

"I know that already," you say wearily. "That's what—"

"What you know about Dimitrius is very limited," says the professor. "I am from the Institute of Theoretical Physics in Copenhagen. If my calculations about Dimitrius are correct, then . . . But if you will come to Copenhagen, I will show you."

"To Copenhagen?" you say.

"If we take the train tonight, we can be there by morning," he says. "It is urgent!"

Turn to page 79.

"A gambler, that's the life for me," you say.

"Well, don't get carried away with it," says T. "You'll have a fixed budget on the amount you can lose."

"And my winnings?" you ask, smiling a bit.

"Your winnings—if any—you can keep, I suppose," say T. "But just remember, that's not why we're sending you. It's very important that we find this Dimitrius in time."

"In time for what?" you ask.

"That's classified information for the moment," says T. "You'll be told all about it when you find Dimitrius. Right now you have a choice between starting your search in Hong Kong or Rio de Janeiro."

If you decide to go to Hong Kong,
turn to page 24.

If you decide to go to Rio de Janeiro,
turn to page 65.

With a piece of chalk you mark the spot on the floor where Dimitrius vanished. Monsieur Pollet has the gallery closed off and the paintings removed. Several of the museum's fire hoses are run into the gallery and aimed at Dimitrius's "time gate."

You, Jacques, and two guards start taking quard shifts round the clock. "I suspect that Dimitrius will be back in the next couple of weeks," you say. "And we'll be here waiting for him!"

It *is* almost two weeks later that things begin to pop. The first sign that something is happening starts on Jacques's shift—just before dawn. You are sleeping on a cot in the small storeroom just off the gallery when a hand shakes you awake. It's Jacques.

"Quick, wake up!" he whispers. "I think we have company."

Turn to page 95.

As you start into the casino Mai Ling waves good-bye and runs down the street. You wave back, wishing you could thank her more.

Inside, the casino is bustling. Every kind of gambling game imaginable is going on. You don't see anyone who looks like Dimitrius. You decide to act the part of a gambler to try to get some information.

You go over to the roulette wheel and place a bet. You win! You try again. Another win! You try a slot machine and hit the jackpot! The chips pour out. You are definitely on a winning streak.

Soon you have a huge pile of gambling chips. You know you should quit while you're ahead, but gambling fever has taken hold of you. Heading back to the roulette wheel, you decide to wager everything on one big gamble.

If you bet on red to win, turn to page 53.

If you bet on black to win, turn to page 94.

"I don't think I can trust you that far," you tell Dimitrius. "You can contact the American government from the headquarters of the harbor police."

"Fly me to my yacht!" Dimitrius demands. "Or else . . ."

"Or else what?" you say. "Shoot if you like, but you'd better know how to fly a helicopter."

Meanwhile Mai Ling has slipped away from the front of the helicopter. Suddenly there is a rush of air as she opens the cargo door.

"What the . . . !" Dimitrius exclaims. "Where is that girl?"

Then there is a loud banging and hammering in the back of the helicopter.

Turn to page 56.

"I don't know, I—"

"But T said that you would cooperate," says the professor in a pleading voice. "I have a car downstairs ready to take us to the train station."

However, the professor's car doesn't go to the train station. Something makes you doze off soon after getting in the car. When you wake up, you are tied up and in a plane. Professor Savenson, if that's his real name, is grinning down at you.

"Sorry about the Copenhagen trick," he says. "Unfortunately I must repeat the experiment I did on Dimitrius at Noginsk. This time my subject will be much younger. I've decided to try it again—using you."

The End

As you try to wake Juan you turn. And what you see behind you turns you weak with fear. A six-foot-high wall of water is crashing down the streambed with the speed of an express train. Quickly you grab Juan and drag him toward the bank. But you're not fast enough. The torrent catches you, hurling you downstream—and into oblivion.

The End

The museum gallery is closed to the public, and during the next two weeks a box of thick, hardened steel is welded together around the spot where Dimitrius vanished. Guards are posted around it night and day.

One morning at four A.M. your phone rings. It's Pollet, reporting that faint noises have started to come from inside the box.

By the time you reach the museum half an hour later, the box is resounding from the force of heavy blows within it. Large bubbles are beginning to appear on the outside of the metal, punched from inside.

"How could anybody or anything be that strong?" exclaims Pollet. *"Mon dieu,* will you look at that!"

Though you can't see anything inside it, the heavy steel box is actually jumping off the floor from the force of the blows.

Turn to page 86.

"Hey! What's going on!" you shout.

There are no door handles on the inside of the car. An opaque glass partition separates you from the driver. You pound on the window for a second before you realize your mistake.

In a panic you open your attaché case and grab your laser pistol to cut your way out. But you are not fast enough. A blast of lethal gas is pumped into the back of the car, and you slump over your attaché case—lifeless.

The End

You signal Juan, and the two of you ease over the side of the truck and drop to the ground. Quietly you slip into the dense jungle growth.

A few seconds later there are loud angry shouts as the kidnappers come to life and start in pursuit. A loud *rat-tat-tat* comes from the road as they spray the jungle with machine-gun fire. Bullets whiz through the trees above you. They must have orders to recapture you alive. They are just trying to scare you—and they are succeeding.

Then you see a narrow path off to one side.

"This way, Juan," you whisper. "I think I see how to get through."

Turn to page 100.

"We go on foot from here," the man with the mustache orders. "Everyone out of the truck— *vamos.*" You and Juan climb out. The truck is pushed off the road and hidden in the thick foliage. Then, with half the guards in front of you and half behind, you start down a jungle trail. Frequently, the men in front have to cut their way through the growth with machetes—long swordlike knives. The jungle heat is so oppressive that you are soon drenched with sweat.

After an hour or so, you come to a wide clearing. Tents are set up around its edge. On the other side of the clearing, a stone pyramid rises out of the jungle in a series of high steps.

Turn to page 90.

"It seems," you say, "that once Dimitrius has begun to return to the present he can't stop the process and vanish back into the future. And while he is slowly rematerializing he has superhuman strength—or at least his shadow has. Also—"

Suddenly the side of the box closest to you starts to glow red-hot—then white. A hole begins to melt in the side, throwing a shower of sparks in all directions. And a ghostly form shoots through the hole so fast that you have no time to jump out of the way.

With a tremendous crash the white-hot deadly apparition splatters you into a thousand fiery pieces and continues on right through the outer wall of the museum—vanishing in a streak of light across the rooftops of Paris.

The End

"What's going on?" Juan says, his voice shaking.

"I wish I knew," you say. "This whole place looks as if it's about to explode. We'd better get out of here—if we can."

You start banging on the door, hoping that one of Sandoz's men will open it. One of them does. Maybe he thinks you know what to do. You and Juan join the men trying to wrestle some of the huge stones out of the stairway.

"It's coming loose!" you holler.

But just as that stone pulls out of the way, several others crash down to take its place. The whole ceiling is now red-hot. It feels as if you're in an oven.

"If we're not blown up," you say, "we're going to be cooked. Let's give these stones one more try."

But one more try is all you get. Somewhere above you Dimitrius expodes with a force of a small atomic bomb. Where you were standing moments before is now the center of a deep crater surrounded by molten rock.

The End

"If you must get to the helicopter, I know how we can come up behind it," says Mai Ling.

She leads you back down the long corridor and out a side door. Two men are carrying boxes and loading them on the helicopter.

"Stay behind me, Mai Ling," you say. "I'm going to try to jump aboard when those men go back inside."

About thirty seconds later you dash across to the helicopter and spring inside the loading door. Mai Ling is right behind you. Inside, you race to the pilot's compartment, and before the startled pilot can react, you knock him unconscious with a blow to the side of the neck, pull him out of his seat, and take his place.

You see from the switches on the control panel that the helicopter is ready for takeoff. You pull back the throttle, and the chopper rises. Down below, men are running out of the villa and shouting up at you. But in a matter of seconds the villa looks as tiny as a postage stamp, and you are flying high above the harbor.

"I guess we're home free," you say.

"Not quite," says a deep voice from the back compartment.

"Oh, no!" exclaims Mai Ling. "I didn't know there was anyone back there."

"There wasn't," says the voice, coming out of a slowly materializing form—a form with a gun in its hand.

Turn to page 47.

The guards direct you to one of the tents, its sides pulled up so that the roof seems to float above the ground like a large sail. In the center of the tent sits a heavy, deeply tanned man with a completely bald head.

"Señor Sandoz!" exclaims Juan. "What are *you* doing here?"

"Doing here?" Sandoz repeats. "This is all part of my operation. I have made one of the greatest archaeological discoveries of all time. And this time your father will not cheat me out of the credit—or the profits. I have you here as my insurance policy. If he doesn't do what I tell him, he may not see you again."

"That's kidnapping!" Juan says angrily.

"Maybe," says Sandoz, "but it won't be if you write your father a letter saying that you have *voluntarily* joined our little expedition. After you do that, I'll even show you the treasure."

Juan looks at you questioningly, hoping you can help him decide what to do.

*If you advise Juan to write the letter,
turn to page 12.*

*If you advise him not to write the letter,
turn to page 110.*

92

Your hand slips down to your attaché case. You take a deep breath and press a button on its side. There is a faint hissing sound. The important thing is for you to hold your breath for the next sixty seconds.

The gunman from the front of the plane comes toward you.

"All right!" he shouts at you. "Get your hands up."

But his order is just a little bit too late. A colorless, odorless, anesthetic gas fills the whole plane. It is effective for exactly sixty seconds. Both gunmen sink to the floor, and the other passengers are soon unconscious. You count to yourself: one thousand one, one thousand two . . . one thousand fifty-nine, one thousand sixty. You gasp for breath.

Turn to page 66.

"Oh, no!" exclaims Danielle. "They're flushing out the tunnel at this time of night? But here's the ladder. We'll be up to the street in no time."

You clip the flashlight to your belt and start up the ladder after her. The roaring is getting louder. You are almost to the top when a kick from Danielle connects with a crushing blow to your head. You fall off the ladder and plummet back into the tunnel just as the wall of water hits.

You don't live to hear Danielle say: "That gets rid of another one of those meddling SSA agents. Now I'll definitely find Dimitrius first."

The End

Black loses! You watch as all your chips are raked in by the house. You've lost almost all the money you came in with plus all that you won. There's just enough change in your pocket to take the ferry back to Lu Chang's.

You make your way toward the ferry, wondering how you're ever going to explain this to T. But before you reach the ferry, someone grabs you from behind. There's no chance to resist. You're pulled into an alley, bound, and gagged. Next weights are tied to your feet. "So you'll sink when we drop you in the harbor," one of your attackers assures you.

Another man laughs. "No professional gambler would have handled a bet like that. Dimitrius spotted this phony right away!"

The End

You hop out of bed and run to your station at the fire hose. At first you see only a faint glimmer in the darkness. Then gradually you see the illuminated outline of a man take shape. You wait until you can clearly recognize Dimitrius.

"Now!" you shout. "Turn on the hoses!"

You and Jacques open your nozzles, and two streams of water pound into the glowing form. The figure doesn't move, but there is a loud hissing as though you had turned your hoses on white-hot metal. A luminous cloud of steam envelops Dimitrius. Then a whirring sound rises above the hiss. The *Venus de Milo* flies away from Dimitrius and strikes the wall on the other side of the gallery. You hope it isn't too badly damaged.

Dimitrius himself is shrinking into a globe of fiery light spinning a few feet off the floor. The strong columns of water seem to vanish as they hit it—as if they were pouring into an open hole.

Then the ball slowly starts to get smaller . . . and smaller. Suddenly there is a bright flash of light, and it vanishes altogether. You and Jacques turn the hoses off.

"Thank you," Pollet says. "Now we no longer have to fear Dimitrius's stealing works of art."

Jacques smiles at you. "I think we have cooled him down for good."

Although you're relieved that Dimitrius is no longer a threat, you have a new worry: Your mission was to bring him back alive.

"We've cooled Dimitrius down, all right," you agree. "Now all I've got to do is cool down T."

The End

When you board, you immediately spot the two men sitting near the middle of the plane. Your seat is at the rear. Sitting next to you is a teenage boy.

"My name is Juan—Juan Morales," he tells you as the plane takes off. "I've been in school in Washington for the past year. Now I'm going home to be with my family."

About an hour later you notice that the two suspicious-looking men have gotten up from their seats. The taller one goes to the front of the plane; the one with the mustache goes past you to the very rear.

Suddenly both men pull guns from their coats— somehow they must have slipped them past the airport metal detectors.

"Now, everybody do what you're told, and no one will get hurt," barks the man in front.

He opens the door to the flight deck, enters, and shuts the door behind him. Soon you hear muffled shouts and threats coming from inside. You look at the man behind you. His gun is aimed at your head.

"Just keep looking straight ahead," he orders.

Your attaché case is at your feet. The question is, How can you maneuver yourself into a position to use it? If you make a wrong move, the man behind you may shoot. On the other hand, this might be your only chance to stop the hijacking.

If you decide to try to get to your attaché case,
turn to page 92.

If you decide that this is too dangerous,
turn to page 34.

You and Juan lie low while Dimitrius gathers up all the gold objects he can carry and then ascends the stairway leading to the surface. All is quiet for a while; then you hear gunfire up above. This is followed by a deep roll of thunder, but not ordinary thunder—the solid stone walls of your cell seem to shake.

Moments later Sandoz's men charge down the stairway into the crypt. You watch them through the peephole. One of them has a flashlight, and in its light you can see them huddled together in the far corner, cringing with fear. There is another roll of thunder, and this time the pyramid walls shake violently. They're still shaking! You notice how hot it is getting in the cell, which was chilly until a few moments ago.

One of Sandoz's men points to the ceiling of the crypt, where a large spot is glowing cherry-red. Several of the men run to the stairway to get out, but at that moment the large blocks of stone above it begin crashing down, sealing all of you underground.

Turn to page 88.

When you come to, you find yourself tied to a stone slab in a dungeon of some sort. A metal band around your skull keeps you from moving your head. Several men are standing over you. A drop of water from somewhere above hits the center of your forehead. Another drop comes . . . then another.

"We will be back in a day," one of the men says. "Then we will see what you wish to tell us."

"Now, wait a minute, I—" you start.

But your captors have vanished. There is nothing but silence—and the faint *plop* of each drop of water as it hits your forehead.

In a few hours you are ready to scream. Each drop feels like a hammer coming down on your head. Then suddenly the water stops. You see a small figure standing in the dim light. A young Chinese girl is holding her hand over your forehead, catching the drops.

Turn to page 103.

Your new route makes the going easier. The shouts of the men chasing you sound farther and farther away. You have been going steadily downhill since you left the main road. Now you come to a wide, dried-up streambed.

"A dry stream in the jungle?" you ask.

"This is probably a runoff channel," Juan says. "My father has told me all about them. Every time it rains, this becomes a torrent—then dries out quickly."

"It looks like a good path to follow," you say. "We could really make time getting away from those kidnappers."

"Maybe," Juan says slowly, "but it might be safer going straight through the jungle."

If you decide to follow the streambed, turn to page 39.

If you decide to keep going straight through the jungle, turn to page 25.

"I think I'd like to get a look at Dimitrius's yacht," you say.

"Good," says Ho. "My friend has a seaplane nearby. Come."

Ho leads you out of the ferry terminal and down to the waterfront. A seaplane floats peacefully at the end of a pier. Ho explains to his friend what you are looking for.

"How will we know which boat it is?" asks Ho's friend. "There are a lot of boats out there."

"Very simple," answers Ho. "The back of the boat has a helicopter pad with a large *D*."

Ho remains behind. You are ten minutes flying time out over the sea to the south, when suddenly the single engine of the small seaplane starts to sputter and then dies completely.

Turn to page 104.

You hear Sandoz fasten a latch on the outside of the cell door. There is a peephole in the center of the door, and Sandoz shines his flashlight through it for a second.

"Pleasant dreams with the Indian ghosts," he says, laughing evilly.

"Do—do you think that there really are ghosts down here?" Juan asks.

"I don't know," you say, "but right now we're better off trying to get some rest, not worrying about ghosts."

Both of you doze off. Some time later, however, a loud banging and rattling in the crypt next door wakes you. The peephole in the door glows with a dim, eerie light.

"It's the ghosts!" whispers Juan.

Through the peephole you see a luminous figure rummaging around among the gold objects, stuffing smaller ones into his pockets and holding some of the larger ones in his arms. Then the figure turns in your direction. You recognize him immediately.

"That's no ghost," you tell Juan. "It's the man I've been looking for—Dimitrius. And now that I've found him, I'm not sure what to do."

"Maybe if we bang on the door, he'll let us out," says Juan.

"No telling what he'll do," you say.

If you decide to bang on the door and attract Dimitrius's attention, turn to page 42.

If you decide to lie low and not let Dimitrius know that you are there, turn to page 97.

"I am Mai Ling," she says. "I must get you out of here before Fang Ti and his men return."

With a knife Mai Ling cuts the ropes binding you to the stone slab and then helps you pull your head out of the ring.

"Quickly, follow me," she says. She leads you up a stone stairway and then down a long corridor. Finally you come to a large kitchen. It is deserted, but you can hear voices nearby.

From somewhere outside you hear the roaring of what sounds like an airplane. There is a small window at the side of the kitchen. You look out. A helicopter is parked nearby, warming up its engines.

"A delivery truck is parked outside," Mai Ling tells you. "It goes to the waterfront to get fish every day at this time. I think we could sneak inside the back of it and get away."

You consider this. "Could you get me to that helicopter over there?" you ask. "I know how to fly one."

"I could try," she says. "It sounds more dangerous than the truck. Whichever you do, you must take me with you."

If you decide to hide in the delivery truck, turn to page 67.

If you try to get to the helicopter, turn to page 89.

"I can't understand this at all," says the pilot. "We have enough gas, and all of my instruments are reading all right. We can glide in for a landing though. That boat you're looking for is right up ahead."

The pilot is right. There is Dimitrius's yacht not far away. The plane seems to drop a little too quickly to suit you, but the pilot pulls back on the stick at just the right time. The plane bounces on the water for a few moments and then comes to a stop—still afloat. A launch is already coming across to you from the yacht.

"Come aboard," a sailor shouts over to you. "Dimitrius has been expecting you."

"Expecting me? How?" you ask.

"You'll have a long time to find out," says the sailor as you step into the launch. "We're sailing for the South Seas in an hour. Dimitrius has instructed me to make things ready for a long-term guest."

"What do you mean by that?" you ask the sailor.

"Dimitrius has found out through his agents how interested you are in him," he says. "He's decided to retire to a remote island hideout and write his autobiography, and he figures you're just the person to help him. It may take a long time, though. Dimitrius has a lot to say."

The End

As you jump back to your feet, two more attackers are on you. One of them snaps a flying kick to the side of your head. It knocks you sideways into the railing. You are stunned for a moment and helpless as the other attacker moves in to deliver a fatal blow. But suddenly he goes flying over the railing, followed by the other. Groggily you look around to see what has saved you. There is only an old Chinese gentleman standing there with a slight smile on his face.

"Thank you, old man," you say. "Or is that a very good disguise?"

"It is not a disguise," he says. "I am eighty-four years old. It was not strength that defeated your attackers but proper application of energy and concentration.

"My name is Ho Wong. I am your Hong Kong contact for the SSA. Excuse the delay, please. I was unavoidably detained."

"Well, better late than never," you say. "Do you know where Dimitrius is?"

"I know two places he might be," Ho answers. "He has a big yacht near Macao. He also owns an island. If you want to find the yacht, I have a friend who can fly you there. For the island, I have another friend—with a small boat."

If you decide to search for Dimitrius's yacht,
turn to page 101.

If you decide to try to find the island,
turn to page 50.

Big Fist lies there stunned and groaning. A large hole has been torn away in his sleeve—but there is no blood! You bend down for a close look. There are a few faint sparks inside the hole, and a sizzling sound like an electrical short circuit.

"They got me in my bionic arm," Big Fist moans. "The electrical circuits are tied into my nervous system. My fist is useless."

High overhead a steel shutter slams over the only window, plunging your prison into darkness.

"I just hope that Jacques can help us," Big Fist groans.

"Jacques? Jacques who?" you ask.

"Your friend Jacques," Big Fist answers. "He sent me to rescue you and warn you about Danielle. I tried to talk to you last night, but something knocked me out."

"I really made a mistake there," you say. "I'm sorry."

"Don't worry about that now," says Big Fist. "The important thing is to get out of here alive."

"There is not much chance of that," a man's voice hisses from the steel shutter. And he's right!

The End

"You're insane, Sandoz," you yell as they drag you up the steep steps of the pyramid.

"We'll see about that," says Sandoz with an evil laugh. "My ancestors—on my mother's side, that is—were good at this. If they could do it, I can do it."

At the top, Sandoz's men stretch you over a large stone—the remains of an ancient altar. Sandoz raises the knife over you.

"You can't do it, Sandoz," you say. "This is the twentieth century, and you are a civilized—"

But you never get to finish the sentence. The knife flashes in the sunlight as it slashes down into your chest.

The End

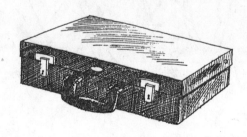

Dimitrius takes one look at you and starts running toward the cable-car station. A car is loading and he jumps aboard—just as he is starting to fade. The other passengers run off screaming. You leave Isabel and manage to jump into the car before the doors close.

It's just you and Dimitrius in the car. The car starts downhill. You are about to try to reason with him when the cable car comes to a jarring stop, suspended in space.

You look back at the station. It has been taken over by the two gangsters. Seconds later you see them running away from the station, and an ear-shattering explosion follows. The explosion severs the cable that your car is suspended from, and you begin falling downward. Behind you, Dimitrius is rapidly fading. Then he is gone. Unfortunately *you* can't fade. The cable car, with you in it, crashes into the mountainside many hundreds of feet below.

The End

"I refuse to write my father a lie," says Juan.

"I see that your friend here not only tried to interfere with my plans on the plane, but is advising you to fight me," snarls Sandoz, glaring angrily at you. "I'll have to demonstrate what I do with those who defy me."

Sandoz signals to his henchmen, and several of them grab you. You stop two of them cold—the first with a jab, and the other with a kick to his head. But you are outnumbered, and they soon have you pinned helplessly, facedown on the ground. They tie your legs together and your hands behind your back.

"Take this fool to the top of the pyramid!" screams Sandoz, pulling a long knife from his belt.

Turn to page 107.

"Okay, Dimitrius," you say. "I'll take a chance and trust you."

Dimitrius points to a white speck far below on the bright blue China Sea. As you head for it the speck expands into a large, very luxurious yacht with a helicopter landing platform at the stern. You land the helicopter, and Dimitrius leads you and Mai Ling below to an elegantly furnished suite.

"Please sit down," Dimitrius says. "Before I contact your government, I'll explain a few things. As you may know, I was used as a guinea pig in a scientific experiment. It had been tried before, but I am the only one it has ever worked on. Why, I don't know.

"I've always been quite ordinary. I gambled a little, collected paintings when I could. Now I am able to travel into the future and return to the present. Sounds wonderful, doesn't it? But the experiment also altered my mind; since then I have been like that Jekyll-and-Hyde character. At times I become someone I don't want to be, and my shadow as I fade in and out of time becomes . . . deadly. I have already destroyed many lives. If your scientists could find a way to change me back, I'd be very grateful."

"I'll do what I can," you promise, and immediately place a call to T in Washington.

Turn to page 37.

Just as the man in black reaches you, you spin around and drop down. His fist, aimed at your head, whistles by your ear. His near miss throws him off-balance for a second—just long enough for you to grab his sleeve and roll backward on the deck. A second later, you let go of your attacker, and he goes sailing over the ferry's railing into the harbor below.

Turn to page 105.

You and Juan lie there in the ditch for the rest of the night. With the first light of morning everything is quiet. Only a thick pall of smoke drifts over the jungle. Together you walk back to where the pyramid once stood. There is no evidence of it now—or of Sandoz's camp. There's only a deep smoldering crater where they had been.

"Well, I guess that takes care of Dimitrius," Juan says.

"And Sandoz, too," you add, "though it's too bad about the treasure."

You and Juan find your way back to a village and call Juan's father in Mexico City. He is overjoyed to hear that Juan is safe and sound so soon after the report of his disappearance. You stay in Mexico City as guest of his family for a few weeks—and a good rest—and then return to Washington for your next assignment.

The End

When you get to the hotel, you pass through the lobby. The desk clerk gives you a nod and points to someone seated nearby with the newspaper *Le Figaro* held up in front of him. You walk over and peer over the paper. A short dark-haired man in a pin-striped suit looks up, startled.

"Zut, alors!" he exclaims. "There you are! I was so worried. I was afraid that the devil in disguise, Danielle, had gotten hold of you. She delayed me long enough earlier so that I missed you at the airport."

"But that agent that met me," you say, "you mean he wasn't—"

"No, he is Danielle's assistant," says the man. "I'm glad to see that you are all right. I have a message from T for you. He says to stay at the airport—well, of course you are not there—but you are to change your cover identity to that of a gambler, and take the next direct flight to Rio de Janeiro."

"I didn't get much chance to be an art collector," you say.

"Well, that's how it goes in our business," says the real agent.

He drives you to the airport—the least he can do—and you buy a ticket for the next plane to Rio.

Turn to page 65.

You feel another stab of pain as you jump to your feet. You realize with horror that the ants have returned. Juan is awake too, yelling and trying frantically to brush the ants off. You both make a desperate dash back down the trail. But it is no use. Dawn will find your two skeletons eaten clean by the ants.

The End

You try to phone Jacques, your contact. He was supposed to be waiting for your call, but there's no answer. You pack the scrambling device back in your attaché case. Sure that something's wrong, you decide to go over to his apartment and see if he's all right.

You catch a cab downstairs and give the driver the address. You know that Jacques lives somewhere on the Cité, as the Parisians call it—the island in the River Seine that holds Notre-Dame Cathedral and is the oldest part of Paris.

Your cab crosses a bridge over the Seine and turns into a dark, narrow street. You get out and walk over to the entrance of Jacques's apartment building. You ring the bell, but there's no answer. As you step back into the street, there is the *pfft* of a silencer from the doorway nearby. You are knocked backward by the bullet. You've walked into an ambush set for your contact. Too bad that you were shot instead.

The End

ABOUT THE AUTHOR

RICHARD BRIGHTFIELD is a graduate of Johns Hopkins University, where he studied biology, psychology, and archaeology. For many years he worked as a graphic designer at Columbia University. He has written *Secret of the Pyramids, The Phantom Submarine, The Dragons' Den,* and *The Secret Treasure of Tibet* in the Choose Your own Adventure series and has coauthored more than a dozen game books with his wife, Glory. The Brightfields and their daughter, Savitri, live in Gardiner, New York.

ABOUT THE ILLUSTRATOR

DON HEDIN was the first artist for the Choose Your Own Adventure series, working under the name of Paul Granger, and has illustrated over twenty-five books in the series. For many years, Mr. Hedin was associated with *Reader's Digest* as a staff illustrator and then as art editor. With his wife, who is also an artist, Mr. Hedin now lives in Oak Creek Canyon, Arizona, where he continues to work as a fine arts painter and illustrator.

CHOOSE YOUR OWN ADVENTURE